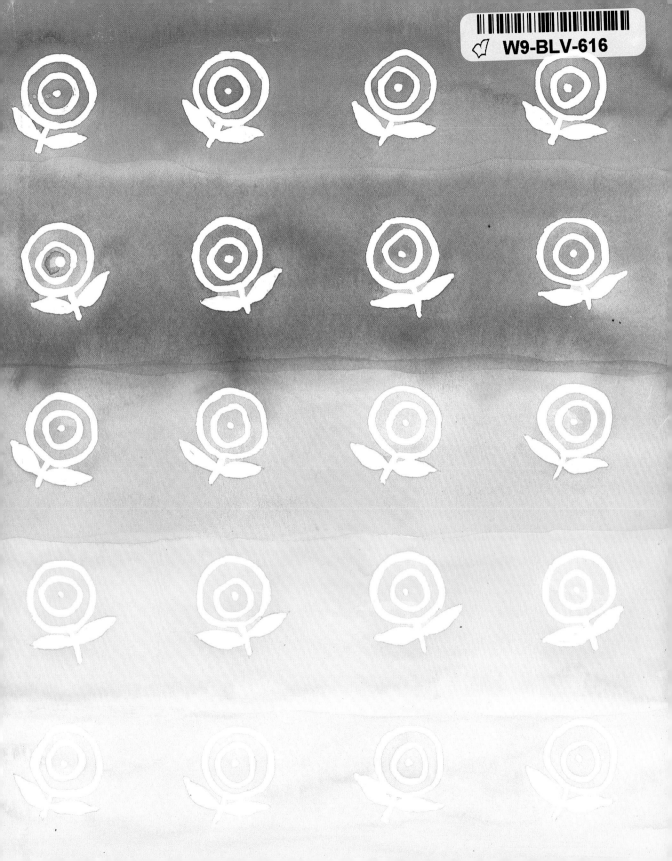

Jessica

by Kevin Henkes

Greenwillow Books

New York

HOLD ON TIGHT, JESSICA.

Watercolor paints and a black pen
were used for the full-color art.
The text type is Monticello.

Jessica
Copyright © 1989 by Kevin Henkes
All rights reserved.

Manufactured in China.
www.harperchildrens.com
For information address HarperCollins Children's Books,
a division of HarperCollins Publishers,
10 East 53rd Street, New York, NY 10022.

First Edition   10 11 12 13 SCP 10 9

Library of Congress Cataloging-in-Publication Data

Henkes, Kevin. Jessica.
"Greenwillow Books."
Summary: Ruthie does everything with her
imaginary friend Jessica; and then on her
first day at kindergarten, she meets a
real new friend with the same name.
[1. Imaginary playmates—Fiction] I. Title.
PZ7.H389Je 1989   [E]   87-38087
ISBN 0-688-07829-X (trade).
ISBN 0-688-07830-3 (lib. bdg.)
ISBN 0-688-15847-1 (pbk.)

GOOD JUMP,
JESSICA!

For
Annie
and
Geri and Mac

WE'RE ALMOST THERE,
JESSICA.

JESSICA IS MY
BEST FRIEND.

Ruthie Simms didn't have a dog.
She didn't have a cat,
or a brother.
or a sister.
But Jessica was the next best thing.

MY TOES ARE COLD TOO, JESSICA.

Jessica went wherever Ruthie went.

To the moon,

to the playground,

to Ruthie's grandma's
for the weekend.

"There is no Jessica,"
said Ruthie's parents.

But there was.

CAREFUL, JESSICA, IT'S HOT.

She ate with Ruthie,

ONCE UPON A TIME, JESSICA...

looked at books with Ruthie,

and took turns stacking blocks with Ruthie, building towers.

If Ruthie was mad, so was Jessica.

If Ruthie was sad,
Jessica was too.

And if Ruthie was glad,

Jessica felt exactly the same.

When Ruthie accidently
spilled some juice,
she said, "Jessica did it,
and she's sorry."

When Ruthie's parents called
a babysitter because they
wanted to go to a movie
one night, Ruthie said,
"Jessica has a stomachache
and wants you to stay home."

And when Ruthie turned five, it was
Jessica's fifth birthday too.

"There is no Jessica,"
said Ruthie's parents.

But there was.

She went to bed
with Ruthie,

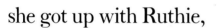

she got up with Ruthie,

and she stayed with Ruthie
all the while in between.

On the night before the first day of
kindergarten, Ruthie's mother said,
"I think Jessica should stay home tomorrow."
Ruthie's father said, "You'll meet a lot
of nice children. You can make new friends."

But Jessica went anyway.

COME ON, JESSICA.
IT'LL BE OKAY.

Jessica wanted to go home so badly that
Ruthie had to hold her hands and whisper
to her. When the teacher announced everyone's
name, Ruthie and Jessica weren't listening.

Jessica crawled
through a tunnel
with Ruthie,

she took a nap
with Ruthie,

and she shared
Ruthie's paintbrush
during art.

When all the children lined up two-by-two
to march to the lavatory, Jessica was
right next to Ruthie.

A girl came up to Ruthie and stood by her side. "Can I be your partner?" she asked. Ruthie didn't know what to say.

"My name is Jessica," said the girl.

"It *is*?" said Ruthie.

 The girl nodded.

"Mine's Ruthie," said Ruthie, smiling.

And they walked down the hallway hand-in-hand.

Ruthie Simms didn't have a dog.
She didn't have a cat,
or a brother,
or a sister.
But Jessica was even better.